Wells Cathedral

QUIRE EMBROIDERIES
ALTAR FRONTALS
AND
VESTMENTS

This book is dedicated to the memory of Janet and Peter James whose idea and dream it was, and to the Very Reverend Richard Lewis whose wish the Millennium Project was.

R.I.P.

Share with us the messages the embroideries contain.

Where to find them.

The needleworkers who stitched them.

Enjoy the Church seasons through the Altar, Frontals and Vestments.

Wells Cathedral

QUIRE EMBROIDERIES
ALTAR FRONTALS
AND
VESTMENTS

Contributors :
Michael Blandford, Neil Bonham, Janet and Peter James, Chris Jenkins,
the Very Reverend Richard Lewis

Compiled by Robin Duijs

Generously funded by the Friends of Wells Cathedral

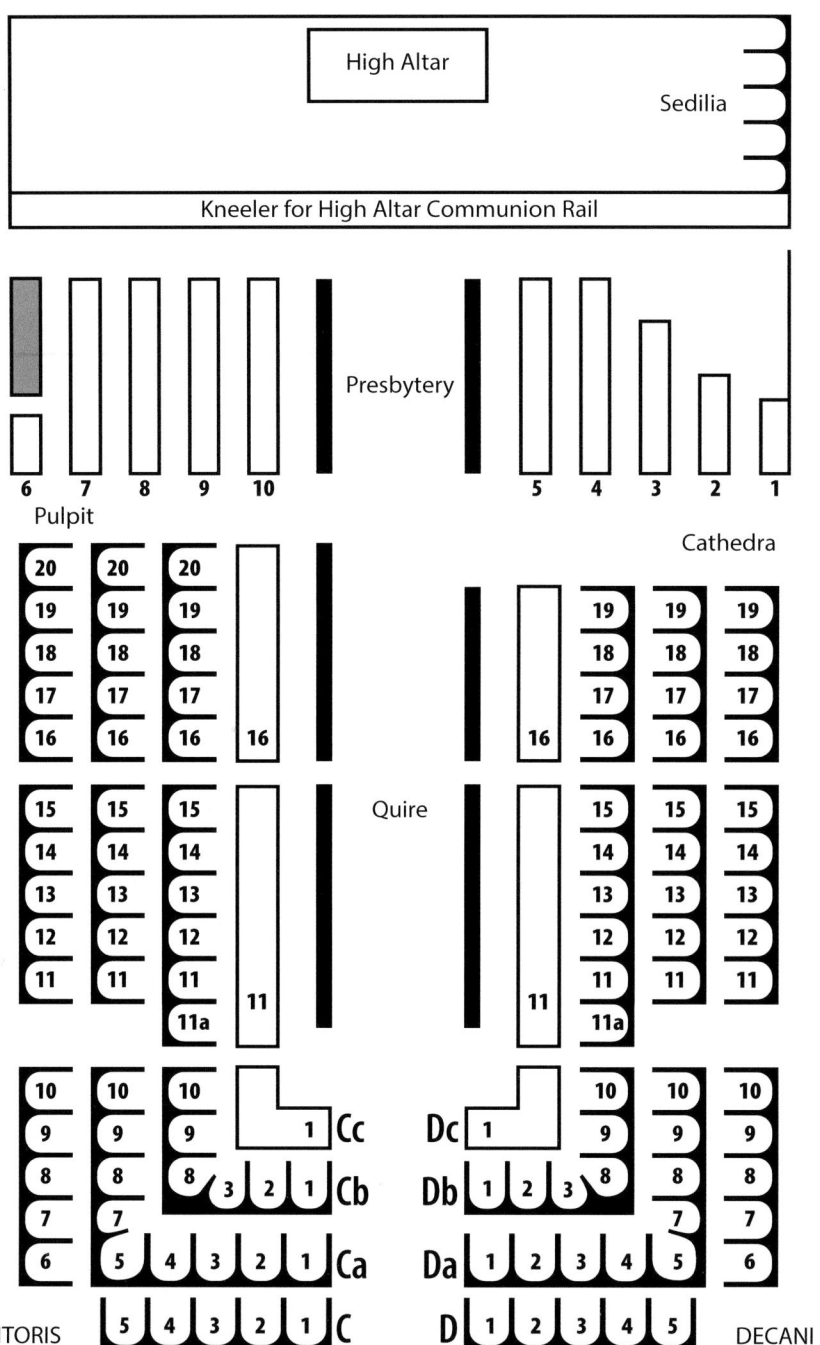

The Hangings in the canons' and prebendaries' stalls at the back are numbered in sequence from the west.

The numbers of the stalls on the south side are prefixed with the letter **D** (decani). The numbers on the stalls on the north side are prefixed with the letter **C** (cantoris).

The substalls take their number from the canon's stall in front of which they stand, and are suffixed with the letter **a** for the upper row, **b** for the lower row and **c** for the front benches.

The description begins with the Dean's stall, and moves from right to left in an anticlockwise direction round the Quire, so that the banners appear in chronological order.

Introduction

The canvas work embroideries in the quire at Wells Cathedral enrich our knowledge and understanding of Christian history and tradition in Somerset and beyond. To look at them is to get a glimpse of a colourful and treasured collection of favourite saints, historical events, legends, kings and bishops, music and organists, ancient manuscripts, favourite parts of the Cathedral and even archaeological features of the Church of the Nativity at Bethlehem.

Canvas work in churches and cathedrals was introduced by Miss Louisa Pesel, an accomplished embroiderer, who, when she visited the newly appointed Bishop of Winchester in the 1920s, offered to furnish his plain and colourless private chapel at Wolvesley Castle with canvas work cushions and kneelers. On seeing them there, the Dean of Winchester wanted the same for Winchester Cathedral. When Dean Malden visited Winchester Cathedral in the early 1930s he, too, wanted a similar project in Wells Cathedral Quire, where it would bring back the rich medieval colour which had been lost after the Reformation.

On his return to Wells, Dean Malden consulted his colleagues and Sir Charles Nicholson, the Cathedral architect, suggested that hangings of an armorial nature relating to the bishops could be placed over the stone backs of the prebendal stalls. A team, to be chaired by Dean Malden, was established to carry out the work. It consisted of Sir Charles Nicholson, Lady Alice Hylton, a talented artist and needlewoman, Miss Isabel Jones, who had retired to Somerset from the Royal School of Needlework, and the antiquarian, Mr. Arthur Vivian Neale. Lady Hylton would make the designs and these would be transferred on to working canvases by Miss Jones. Mr Neale would assist in researching heraldic aspects of the project. Later, a committee was set up and regular meetings took place.

A measure of financial support was given by The Friends of Wells Cathedral which Dean Malden had inaugurated in 1933. The first designs were ready by 1938 and the work began.

Over a hundred volunteer needleworkers, of whom seven were men, were recruited, using advertisements in parish magazines throughout the diocese. Sessions were arranged to give instruction on the stitches to be used, and prospective candidates were required to embroider a test piece.

One of the first decisions was to identify the wide range of materials to be used. The embroideries were to be worked on Winchester canvas in wool and silk, using a wide range of canvas work stitches to suit the designs, with, in some cases, the addition of gold threads, beads, sequins, small pearls and jewels. Wools with vegetable dyes were selected in preference to aniline dyes, as they were washable and less likely to fade. The needleworkers had not got very far when the Second World War broke out and this slowed the work considerably. Supplies of materials were purchased in case of shortage and others were donated. By 1941, the first seven banners were in place and the banners, seats and runners were complete by 1952. It was not an end to the work: projects are still continuing until the present time.

The embroideries may be considered in various parts, as follows:

- The Throne.
- The Banners.

There are thirty-nine banners or hangings. Five of these hang in the corners of the quire above the seats of the five residentiary canons. This seating arrangement follows that of cathedrals of the 'Old Foundation' i.e. those cathedrals which have always been served by secular canons and not by monks. In cathedrals of the 'New Foundation', i.e. those which, until the sixteenth century, were served by monks, the residentiary canons sit together at the west end of the choir. The residentiary canons comprise the Dean, the Precentor, the Chancellor, the Treasurer and the Archdeacon of Wells and, with four lay prebendaries, they form the Chapter of Wells Cathedral. These banners have gold backgrounds.

The other thirty four banners have backgrounds which are red and blue alternately. Two of them hang above the seats of the Archdeacons of Bath and Taunton, and the remaining thirty two banners, with red and blue backgrounds, commemorate some of the bishops. Although there are some exceptions, they are placed in chronological order round the Quire in an anti-clockwise direction. Facing east and beginning at the south west corner of the Quire, next to the Dean's banner, is that of Bishop Drokensford, 1309–29. They end with that of Bishop Wynne Willson, 1921-37, which is next to that of the Precentor in the north west corner. Each of the banners has the bishop's name, the dates of his episcopate, his arms, a mitre or a cardinal's hat and some reference to his background or historical interest. There are, however, some exceptions.

- The backs, seats and runners of the substalls.
- The presbytery bench runners.
- The High Altar kneeler and the sedilia seats.

Left Panel

Centre Panel

Right Panel

Cushion on the reading desk

The Bishop's Throne

The Centre Panel

In the centre is a bejewelled figure of St Andrew which is taken from an ancient painted wooden screen at St Helen's Church, Ranworth, Norfolk.

Above St Andrew are the arms of the see of Bath and Wells, impaling those of Bishop Francis Underhill who was bishop at the time the embroideries were being worked.

At the foot – left, it reads *Alicia Domina Hylton delineavit MCMXLI*, and right, *Leonora Jenner acu effecit MCMXLII*.

The Left Panel

From the top down:

The arms of the see: the cross of St Andrew.

The arms of Canterbury Cathedral showing a pallium, a scarf of white wool, originally sent to newly appointed archbishops by the Pope. Both Bishop Athelm, D13a and St Dunstan, D16a, are seen wearing a pallium on their embroideries.

The Dragon of Wessex.

The Danish Raven, a reminder of King Alfred's battles with the Danes. He finally beat them at the battle of Edington and the Treaty of Wedmore was signed in 878 (see D18b).

King Alfred's Jewel – An aestal or handle of a pointer dug up in Petherton Park in 1693. Alfred was an educator and he instructed his bishops to teach their clergy about pastoral care, from a book of Pope Gregory the Great which he had translated (see Chancellor's banner D18). The jewel can be seen in the Ashmolean Museum in Oxford.

The arms of King Alfred (traditional).

The Dragon of Somerset.

The arms of Edward the Elder, the son of King Alfred, who founded the bishopric of Somerset in 909.

The Dragon of Wessex.

The arms of Glastonbury Abbey (see C11a).

The Right Panel

From the top down:

The arms of the See: the cross of St Andrew.

The arms of Canterbury Cathedral.

The Dragon of Somerset.

The arms of King Arthur.

Cross with a motto of Emperor Constantine *In hoc signo vinces* ('By this sign you shall conquer').

The arms of Glastonbury Abbey.

The Dragon of Wessex.

The arms of the see of Sherborne. King Ina founded the bishopric in 705. Wells was in Sherborne Diocese until 909, when it too, became a bishopric.

The Harp of St Aldhelm (see C8a).

The arms of the Saxon kings, used today in the arms of the Dean and Chapter of Westminster Abbey.

At the foot of the side panels – *Alicia Domina Hylton delineavit*. And, *Mildred Alice Carr effecit*.

The Desk Cushion

The desk cushion was worked by Miss Elizabeth Underhill in memory of her brother, Bishop Francis Underhill, who died suddenly in 1943.

D1 The Dean

D2 The Archdeacon of Taunton

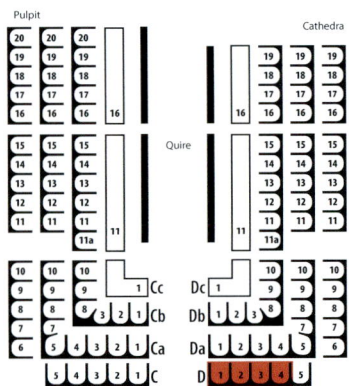

D3 John Drokensford 1309-29

D4 John Harewell 1367-86

The Banners

D1 The Dean

Centre: The arms of Dean Malden, 1933–50, impaling the arms of the Dean and Chapter, with his family motto below.

Top left and right: The arms of earlier deans.

Bottom left: The arms of Eton College and right: The arms of King's College Cambridge. Dean Malden was alumnus of both Colleges.

In corners: Rose-en-soleil (badge of Edward IV). In border: Three daisies on a turf: (badge of Lady Margaret Beaufort).

Bottom: In Latin: 1949 is the date the embroidery was placed in the Quire.

D2 The Archdeacon of Taunton

The arms of the borough of Taunton with the word *Defendamus* (let us defend).

The peacock, featured on the crest, is taken from the design on the vase of the town's 13th century seal.

The mural crown refers to Taunton Castle.

The castles in the corners indicate that there has been a fortress in Taunton since the eighth century. At the bottom, the capital T in a barrel forms a rebus TAU-IN-TUN.

D3 Bishop John Drockensford, 1309-29.

The medlar tree in the diamond tells the tale that the bishop gave some of his garden, adjoining the newly built Lady Chapel and St Andrew's Well, to Canon Michael of Easton, but a path of eight feet wide was reserved to give the bishop access to the medlar tree.

The handcuffs refer to his jail, first mentioned in 1329. His tomb is in St Katherine's Chapel.

D4 Bishop John Harewell, 1367-86.

Below his arms are two hares drinking from a well: a rebus.

At the bottom: the upper part of the south west tower towards which the bishop paid two thirds of the cost. It is used as the belfry, and he gave two bells.

The Prince of Wales' feathers with the motto, *Ich Dien*, tell that he was chaplain and Chancellor to Edward the Black Prince.

D5 Nicholas Bubwith 1407-24

D6 Thomas Beckington 1443-65

D7 Robert Stillington 1466-91

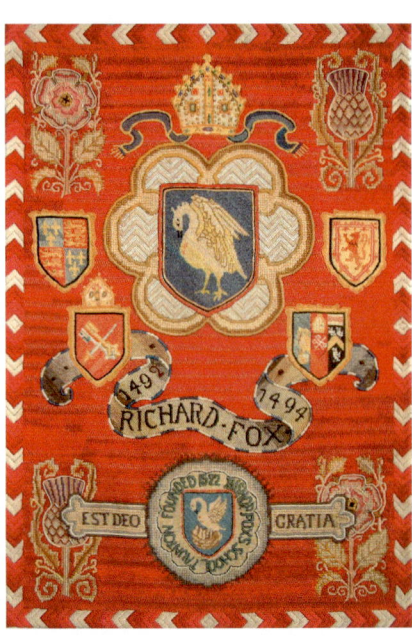

D8 Richard Fox 1492-94

D5 Bishop Nicholas Bubwith, 1407-24.

His arms can be seen in stained glass in the Cathedral Library, which he funded, and on the door of the Close Chapel. Holly leaves forming part of his arms appear on his chantry chapel in the nave and also on the north west tower, where there is a statue of him. He also founded the Bubwith Almshouses in Wells. The bag shows the royal arms of Henry IV. Bubwith was Treasurer of England, 1407-8.

D6 Bishop Thomas Beckington (Bekynton), 1443-65.

The angels around his arms are taken from his tomb. Bottom left and right: his initials, 'T' and 'B'. In the 'T' the Arms above: Winchester College, and below: the see of Winchester. In the 'B', above: Eton College, and below: Lincoln College. Between the 'T' and 'B': his rebus. In Wells, he built the Penniless Porch, Chain Bridge, Brown's Gate, Bishop's Eye, the 'New Works' in the Market Place, and he supplied piped water from springs in the palace garden to the City.

D7 Bishop Robert Stillington, 1466-91.

Robert Stillington was Lord Chancellor of England from 1462-73. He built a second Lady Chapel projecting from the cloister. This was a mortuary chapel to house his tomb. It was pulled down in 1552.

D8 Bishop Richard Fox, 1492-94.

The Bishop adopted the pelican 'in her piety' for his Arms. Left, from the top down: Rose of England, royal arms of England, arms of the see of Winchester, thistle of Scotland. Right from the top down: Thistle of Scotland, royal arms of Scotland, arms of Corpus Christi College, Oxford (which he founded), the rose of England. Bottom: Arms of Bishop Fox's School in Taunton, which he founded in 1522.

D9 Oliver King 1495-1503

D10 Hadrian de Costello 1504-18

D11 Thomas Wolsey 1518-23

D12 William Knight 1541-47

D9 Bishop Oliver King, 1495-1503.

To the left and right of arms: Lilies from the arms of Eton College (he was a scholar there about 1445). He was a supporter of Henry VII and the monogram on either side is taken from his tomb in Westminster Abbey. The portcullis, a badge of the Beaufort family, represents the line of Henry's mother, Lady Margaret Beaufort, through whom Henry inherited the throne. Shells in the corners are taken from his arms. See C20.

D10 Cardinal Hadrian de Costello, Bishop 1504-18.

Hadrian's arms are surmounted by a cardinal's hat. He was Italian and sent to England by the Pope in 1489 as collector of 'Peter's Pence'. In 1492 he became Henry VII's ambassador in Rome. He was made Cardinal in 1503 and Bishop of Bath and Wells in 1504. As he was in Rome most of the time, the diocese was run by a compatriot, Polydore Vergil, Archdeacon of Wells. (see C18a).

D11 Cardinal Thomas Wolsey, Bishop 1518-23.

Wolsey's Arms are surmounted by a cardinal's hat. Behind the shield are a pastoral staff, an archiepiscopal and a legatine cross. He became papal legate, the direct representative of the Pope in England. He does not seem to have visited Wells. He was Bishop of Lincoln and Archbishop of York at the same time and only surrendered Bath and Wells when granted Durham (a fine example of pluralism).

D12 Bishop William Knight, 1541-47.

Below his Arms are the words *Preache thou the Worde*, which is part of the inscription on the pulpit in the nave, under which he is buried. Before he became a bishop he was Henry VIII's chaplain and ambassador to the court of Maximilian I. Henry granted him a coat of arms for his services, and this is also why the rose of England and the imperial crown form a pattern in the background.

D13 William Barlow 1548-54

D14 Gilbert Bourne 1554-60

D15 Gilbert Berkeley 1560-81

D16 John Still 1593-1608

D13 Bishop William Barlow, 1548-53.

Barlow was both evangelical and anti-catholic. He resigned his see when Mary Tudor came to the throne, and tried to escape from England but was caught and imprisoned in the Tower. This is reflected in the banner, where two pomegranates, Mary's badge, are linked by a chain. On release he fled to Germany. After the accession of Queen Elizabeth I in 1559, he assisted in the consecration of Matthew Parker as Archbishop of Canterbury and became Bishop of Chichester. He was the first married bishop and he had five daughters.

D14 Bishop Gilbert Bourne, 1554-59.

Bourne, who had catholic leanings, was appointed to the see by Mary Tudor, who made him President of the Council of Wales. The Court of the President and Council of Wales had been established by Henry VII, who had intended to make his son Arthur, the Prince of Wales, its president. At the top of the banner are a Tudor rose and a pomegranate (Mary's badge). At the bottom is a Welsh dragon. Bishop Bourne was deprived of his see by Elizabeth I.

D15 Bishop Gilbert Berkeley, 1560-81.

Berkeley, a protestant, was in exile in Frankfurt during Mary's reign. He was appointed to the see by Elizabeth I in 1560. In Wells, it is said that his wife encouraged the persecution of the Bourne family and that he had problems with Dean Turner over his attempts to enforce uniformity. His tomb is in the North Quire Aisle of the Cathedral. The scrolls round the mitres on the banner read *VIXI, I have lived*, and *LVXI, I have seen the light*. The Roman letters, as numbers added together, total 83, the age at which he died?

D16 Bishop John Still, 1593-1608.

John Still spent thirty years at Cambridge and was described as "an excellent philosopher, a reasonable good historian, a learned divine and a wise man". The arms round his arms, from top right, clockwise, are those of Cambridge University, St John's College (Master 1574-7), Trinity College (Master 1577-93), and Westminster Abbey, where he was prebendary. The motto, translated, reads *He hath dispersed abroad and given to the poor*. Psalm 112 v.9. His tomb is near the entrance to the Chapter House steps.

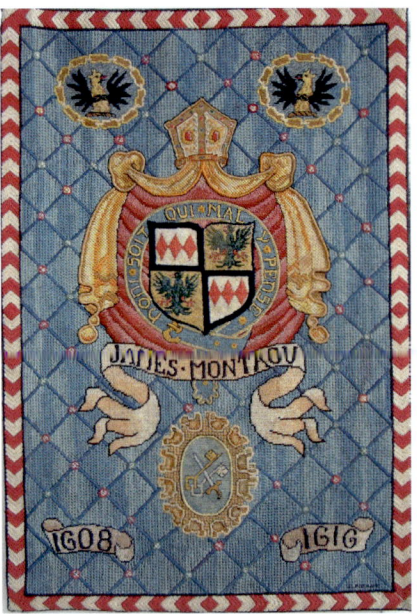

D17 James Montague 1608-16

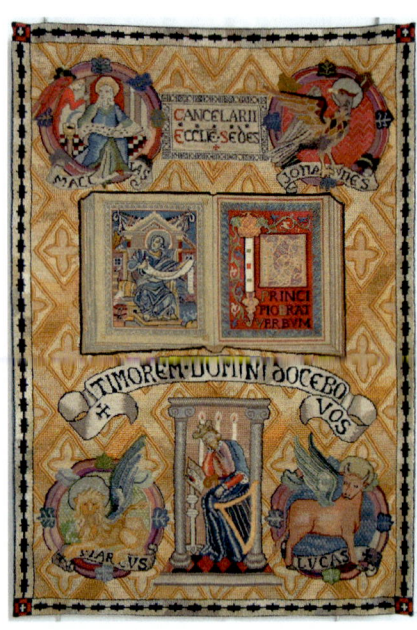

D18 The Chancellor

D19 The Archdeacon of Wells

C20 The Archdeacon of Bath

D17 Bishop James Montague, 1608-16.
Bishop of Bath and Wells, afterwards being translated to Winchester. The shield round his arms is encircled by the Garter (the Bishop of Winchester is traditionally Prelate of the Garter). He repaired the Bishop's Palace in Wells and restored the nave of Bath Abbey, where he is buried, and where he presented a fine stone pulpit. It seems that he began the tradition of sending a sprig of the Glastonbury Thorn to the monarch in December each year. At the bottom centre of the banner are the arms of Bath Abbey.

D18 The Chancellor
The Chancellor is one of the canons of the Chapter of Wells Cathedral. The banner is a job description illustrating some of his responsibilities: teaching and the library. In the centre is a bible, open at the beginning of St John's Gospel. The design is taken from a ninth century manuscript of the School of Rheims and is kept in the Pierpoint Morgan Library in New York. Below the bible are the words *I will teach you the fear of the Lord*. Psalm 34 v.11. In the four corners are the symbols of the four evangelists. At the bottom is King Alfred, a literary man. (See Throne left hand panel).

D19 The Archdeacon of Wells
The Archdeacon of Wells is also one of the canons of the Chapter of Wells Cathedral. In the centre are the arms of the City of Wells. Below is the seal of King John dated May 9th 1202, the date when he gave the City its charter. Below again, the obverse of a seal showing King John seated on his throne, with the words *John by the Grace of God King of England and Lord of Ireland*. Below on either side, the seal of the borough of Wells. Centre sides, the royal arms of King John. Top sides, the arms of the see of Bath and Wells.

C20 The Archdeacon of Bath
He is one of three archdeacons of the see (the others being those of Taunton and Wells). In the centre are the arms of Bath Abbey: the keys of St Peter and the sword of St Paul. At either side at the top is an olive tree. Below, there are angels climbing ladders, as can be seen carved in the stone of the west front of the Abbey. Around the shield are the words: *Let a king restore the church, let an olive establish the crown*. This refers to a dream which Oliver King (Bishop 1495-1053), is said to have had. He saw it as a divine command to rebuild the ruined Bath Abbey and also his support of Henry VII, who became king after the battle of Bosworth Field (see D9).

C19 The Treasurer

C18 William Laud 1626-28

C17 Arthur Lake 1616-26

C16 Walter Curle 1629-32

C19 The Treasurer

He is one of the five canons of the Chapter of Wells Cathedral. This embroidery too, is a job description. The Treasurer is responsible for the treasures of the Cathedral, which includes the embroideries. He is not responsible for the money. In the centre are two angels, one holding a paten and the other a chalice. Below, translated from Latin is, *He bringeth forth out of his treasures things new and old.* Matthew ch.13 v.52.

C18 Bishop William Laud, 1626-28.

William Laud was at Oxford University for thirty years. A 'high Anglican', he incurred the wrath of many puritanical clergy who considered him to be a papist. They banned the prayer book, and tried to rid the churches of 'popish' symbols and idols, including altar statues, stained glass and organs. Laud, who hated disorder, wanted a railed-off altar, furnished with decent ornaments at the east end of the church. He also wanted the prayer book to be used and vestments to be worn. Encouraged by Charles I, he became Bishop of St David's (1621), Bath and Wells (1626), London (1628) and Archbishop of Canterbury (1633). He never visited Wells, but relied on Bishop William Piers (1632-70) to implement his policies. Bishop Laud was beheaded in 1645. In the embroidery, two C's surmounted by a crown tell of his devotion to Charles I and they have the Arms of St John's College, Oxford, between them.

C17 Bishop Arthur Lake, 1616-1626.

Arthur Lake was educated at Winchester College and New College, Oxford where he became Warden in 1613. An academic, it is thought that he was involved in the translation of the King James Bible. He was an able preacher and a disciplinarian, but diligent when dealing with his clergy and caring and considerate in regard to their families. He died in 1626 and is buried in the South Quire aisle of Wells Cathedral. Below his Arms on the embroidery are the words, *All wisdom cometh from the Lord.* In the field are the rose of England and the thistle of Scotland, dimidiated and surmounted by a crown.

C16 Bishop Walter Curle, 1629-32.

Walter Curle succeeded his friend Leonard Mawe as Bishop of Bath and Wells, having previously been Dean of Lichfield, Bishop of Rochester and chaplain and almoner to the King. Through Laud's influence he was translated to Winchester in 1632, where he remained for fifteen years. A staunch royalist and high Anglican, he was forced to flee his palace by the advancing army of Oliver Cromwell and was deprived of his see. He retired from public life to Soberton, where he died in 1647. His banner shows, to the left and right of his arms the monogram, *Carolus Rex.* Below, are the dimidiated rose of England and thistle of Scotland to represent the first two Stuart kings (see C11).

C15 Robert Creyghton 1670-72

C14 Peter Mews 1673-84

C13 Thomas Ken 1685-91

C12 Richard Kidder 1691-17

C15 Bishop Robert Creyghton, 1670-72.

Robert Creyghton, a royalist and academic, became Treasurer of Wells in 1633, where he stayed until 1645, at which time Parliament forced residentiary canons to leave. He retired to Oxford to become chaplain to Charles I, then to Charles II in exile. After the Restoration he became Dean of Wells, then, in 1670, Bishop . He gave the stained glass in the west window and the brass lectern in the retroquire. He died in 1672 and his tomb is in Corpus Christi Chapel. The embroidery shows capital C's with a crown above, to mark his close association with Charles II. The oak leaves and acorns remind us that the king escaped capture after the battle of Worcester in 1651 by hiding in an oak tree.

C14 Bishop Peter Mews, 1673-1684.

Peter Mews was a royalist who served in the army for many years and was known as the 'Bombardier Bishop'. His portrait shows a black patch on his cheek, which is said to cover a wound acquired at the battle of Naseby. He was translated to Winchester in 1684 and in the following year, after the outbreak of the Monmouth Rebellion he volunteered his services to King James II. At Sedgemoor, he used his own horses to draw the royal cannon to a place where he could successfully direct their fire. He died in 1706 and is buried in Winchester Cathedral. Cannon and cannonballs are seen in the background of the embroidery, and below his arms is a medal with the words, *James II by the Grace of God King of England, Scotland, France and Ireland*.

NB. The banner has the wrong date (1685). 1684 is actually correct.

C13 Bishop Thomas Ken, 1685-91.

On this embroidery we read in the scroll above his arms, *A beloved shepherd, a saintly character*. Below are two angels holding a scroll which quotes from one of his famous hymns. Below again is a medal showing a church founded upon a rock, with the words *Unmoved, victorious*: reflecting his strong adherence to church principles. Bishop Ken began all his letters with the words, *All Glory be to God*, and this is seen at the bottom. In 1688, James II tried to override church law, and Bishop Ken, with seven other bishops, was committed to the Tower for their refusal to co-operate. In 1691 he refused to take an oath of allegiance to William and Mary and he was deprived of the bishopric. He died at Longleat in 1711 and is buried at Frome.

C12 Bishop Richard Kidder, 1691-1703.

Richard Kidder reluctantly accepted the bishopric after Ken had been deprived. He has been described as rather a pathetic figure who lacked a sense of humour. Nevertheless, he survived the dangerous days through which the Church of England passed under Charles II, James II and William and Mary. The embroidery shows the arms of the see impaling those of Kidder. In the corners are the four winds, alluding to the great storm of 1703 when the bishop and his wife were killed by a chimney stack which was blown through the roof of the Palace. They are both buried near the entrance to the Chapter House steps.

C11 George Hooper 1704-27

C10 Edward Willes 1743-73

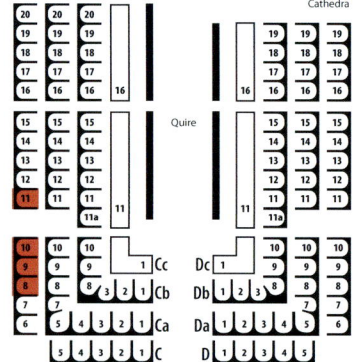

C9 John Wynne 1727-43

C8 Richard Beadon 1802-24

C11 Bishop George Hooper, 1704-27.

George Hooper was a close friend of Bishop Ken. He was chaplain to Princess Mary in The Hague. He had high church beliefs and was disliked by William of Orange (a staunch Calvinist), who declared that Hooper would never be a bishop. After William's death and Kidder's fatal accident in 1703, Queen Anne offered Hooper the see of Bath and Wells, which he accepted with Ken's blessing. He was a popular, caring and successful bishop. An academic, he gave some valuable books, written mainly in Hebrew, to the Cathedral library. The embroidery shows four sprays of oranges, relating to his time spent in Holland. He had no family arms, but devised his own. The dimidiated rose and thistle used as a badge by James I and Charles I, represent the union of England and Scotland. Hooper died in 1727 and he is buried in Wells Cathedral.

C10 Bishop Edward Willes, 1743-73.

The quills on this embroidery tell that Willes was decipherer to King George I. As a student in Oxford, he was taught decoding skills and is said to have had successful careers in the Church and as a decipherer. One such success was achieved between 1719 and 1722 when he decoded communications between Bishop Atterbury of Rochester and Jacobites abroad. This led to Atterbury being convicted and banished to the continent. Willes agreed to become Bishop of St David's in 1742, only when his son had become competent at decoding. In 1743, he was translated to Bath and Wells. A caring man, he built additional almshouses adjacent to the Bubwith almshouses in Wells which are still lived in today. He died in 1773 and is buried at Westminster Abbey.

C9 Bishop John Wynne, 1727-43.

John Wynne came from North Wales. He graduated from Jesus College, Oxford, where in 1712, he was elected Principal. In 1714, George I appointed him as Bishop of St Asaph, and it was here that he gave generously towards repairs of the cathedral following a storm. He became increasingly unpopular at Oxford as his attention was divided between the two posts and he resigned as Principal on his marriage in 1720. In 1727, he was translated to the See of Bath and Wells. He was a botanist and bought Soughton estate in Northop in 1743, where he created magnificent gardens. He died there in 1743 and is buried at Northop Church. The embroidery shows a knot garden with a variety of flowers.

C8 Bishop Richard Beadon, 1802-24.

Richard Beadon was born in Devon. After graduating from St John's College, Cambridge, he later became a fellow and tutor there. He was also public orator to the university. In 1771, Beadon was elected Master of Jesus College, Cambridge. The arms of Jesus College can be seen on the left hand side of the embroidery and the arms of St John's College on the right. In 1789, George III made him Bishop of Gloucester. Thirteen years later, he was translated to Bath and Wells. At Wells, he redesigned the north wing of the Bishop's Palace, creating a third storey where there had been two. The mitre on the embroidery is a piece of appliquéd satin from a dress worn by Mrs Beadon when she was presented at the court of George III. Bishop Beadon died in 1824 and is buried in Wells Cathedral.

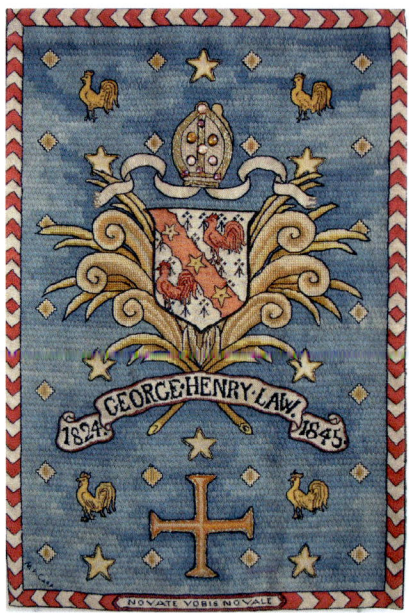

C7 Bishop George Henry Law 1824-45

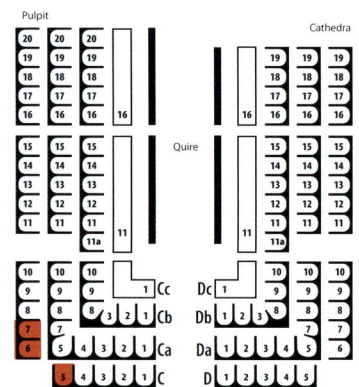

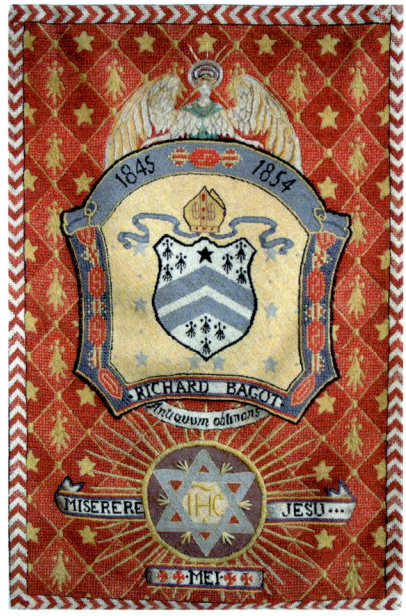

C6 Richard Bagot 1845-54

C5 Robert Eden - Lord Auckland 1854-69

C7 Bishop George Henry Law, 1824-45.

George Henry Law was translated to Wells from Chester where he had been bishop. He was active and practical in Chester and in Wells. He was interested in old glass, and bought a wagon load of stained glass from Rouen which can be seen in various places, including Wells Cathedral and Palace. In 1830, three labourers were condemned to death at Wells Assizes for setting fire to ricks at Ken, and Law, deeply upset by this, bought land on the Mendips to be used for allotments for Priddy labourers. Reference is made to this in the words at the bottom of the embroidery *Break up your fallow ground*. In 1831, Law was one of twenty-one bishops who opposed the Electoral Reform Bill. Riots took place in Bristol, and the Cathedral and Bishop's Palace there were damaged. As he was travelling to Bedminster to consecrate a new church there, a mob stoned Law's carriage and he hurried back to Wells to the safety of the Palace. According to tradition, Law, as Bishop of Bath and Wells, supported Queen Victoria at her coronation in 1837. At the ceremony he turned over two pages in error and the Queen failed to make all her promises but after intervention from the sub-dean, she had to return in order complete them. In 1840, Law was instrumental in the establishment of Wells Theological College. Law and his son, the Archdeacon of Wells, who was also rector of Weston super Mare, were involved in Weston's transformation from a sleepy fishing village into a thriving holiday resort. They provided the site for a town hall and paid for its erection. In Wells, Law undertook repairs to the Palace and in 1845, landscaped the gardens there. The Bishop died at Banwell in 1845 and is buried in Wells Cathedral.

C6 Bishop Richard Bagot, 1845-54.

Richard Bagot was Bishop of Oxford from 1829-1845, where he had problems with the Oxford Movement, which seemed ultimately to lead to Anglo-Catholicism. This troubled him deeply and at his own request he was translated to Bath and Wells in 1845, when the see had become vacant. At Wells he had a breakdown and was ill for some time. He made many alterations to the Bishop's Palace. He died in 1854 and is buried in the Chapel of Blithfield Hall, the seat of the Bagot family. The embroidery shows the family motto below his Arms, *Maintaining what is ancient*. At the bottom, are two equilateral triangles, which symbolise the Holy Trinity surrounding the monogram *IHC* and the words around it, *Jesus have mercy on me*.

C5 Bishop Robert John Eden (Lord Auckland), 1854-69.

Bishop Eden was translated to Bath and Wells from Sodor and Man, where he had been bishop since 1847. Eden was moderate in his views, but had high church leanings. He retired in 1869 and died at the Bishop's Palace the following year. He is buried in the Palm churchyard at Wells Cathedral. One of his daughters taught the swans in the Palace moat to ring a bell. The embroidery has a mitre above his arms but not a coronet, since the rank of a bishopric is higher than that of a hereditary barony. On each side, instead of the supporters appropriate to a noble family, there are ears of corn, reproduced from sheaves on the arms. The ermine mantle behind the shield is that of a peer of the realm. The keys of St Peter and the sword of St Paul, from the arms of Bath Abbey, can be seen below the shield. The scallops in the field are taken from his arms.

C4 Arthur Hervey 1869-94

C3 Kennion 1894-1921

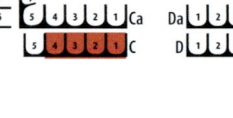

C2 Wynne Willson 1921-37

C1 The Precentor

C4 Bishop Lord Arthur Charles Hervey, 1869-94.

Bishop Hervey was the fourth son of the first Marquis of Bristol. He was also the uncle of Lady Hylton, who designed the Quire embroideries. He was popular and had great concern for the people of Wells, where he founded Cottage Hospital (1874), the Coffee Tavern and Red Lion Club (1882), and the Recreation Ground (1887). He published many theological books, sermons and pamphlets and was a moderate evangelical, once publicly rebuking a priest-vicar for encouraging the congregation to make use of the sign of the Cross. He also refused to institute a clergyman to a benefice on grounds of habitual intemperance, and became involved in a long and costly litigation. Bishop Hervey died 1894, is buried in Camery Garden and has a cenotaph in the south quire aisle. The embroidery shows the arms of the Hervey family supported by two *ounces*, or black leopards.

C2 Bishop St John Basil Wynne Willson, 1921-37.

After graduating from St John's College, Cambridge, he taught classics. He was ordained in 1904 and continued to teach, becoming Master of Marlborough College from 1911-16, after which he became Dean of Bristol. He was consecrated Bishop of Bath and Wells in 1921. He was caring and generous in relieving the financial worries of clergy and others in need. After retiring through ill health in 1937 he died in 1946. At the Diocesan Conference, members recalled *the Bishop's wise wit and witty wisdom whereby a dull matter of necessary diocesan routine was lit by a new and humorous brilliancy and often embellished with a most apt and unexpected quotation from Holy Scripture*. A monogram of his initials, surmounted by a mitre (he had no arms), can be seen on his embroidery and below this, the arms of Marlborough College. On either side, is a basil plant.

C3 Bishop George Wyndham Kennion, 1894-1921.

George Kennion was appointed Bishop of Adelaide in 1883. Whilst on leave in England in 1894, he met the Prime Minister, Lord Rosebery, an old school friend, who appointed him Bishop of Bath and Wells, to succeed Bishop Hervey, who had recently died. In 1907, the privately-owned Glastonbury Abbey was put up for sale by auction. Kennion, anxious that this cradle of Christianity in England should not fall into alien hands, became instrumental in securing it for the Church of England. The millenary of the see in 1909 included a royal visit and he was deeply involved in the celebrations. Bishop Kennion was known for his excellent sermons. He was approachable, got on well with people from all walks of life and had a special interest in Sunday schools and youth organisations. In 1921 ill-health caused him to retire and he died in 1922. In his embroidery the kangaroo and Southern Cross reflect his connection with Australia. At the foot is the monogram XP (the *CHI RHO*), Jesus' initials in Greek, which was used by the Roman Emperor Constantine, 306-7, himself a Christian. (See Throne right side panel).

C1 The Precentor

The Precentor is in charge of the music in the Cathedral and this responsibility is reflected in the embroidery. In the centre is the figure of King David playing his harp and above him on either side there is an angel, chiming bells. Below David, with a musical stave between them, are two seated musicians playing stringed instruments. Below them are choristers singing *Gloria in Excelsis Deo*. The designs of figures of King David and the musicians have been taken from an ancient psalter thought to have been written around 1170 by a house of English Augustinian canons in the diocese of York.

D1a

D2a

D3a

D4a

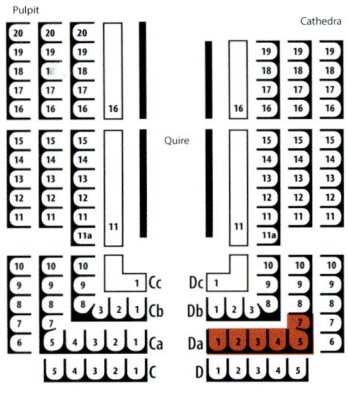

D5a

D7a

The Seats

D1a
A conventionalised rose.

D2a
The Vision of Saint Andrew. When Andrew was a prisoner in Athens, before he was martyred, he had a vision of the Holy Cross. The inscription on the seat back is taken from a hymn, written in the twelfth century by Adam de Saint Victor, which translated reads, *Hail sign of Glory! Hail, Holy sign of Victory! Thus spake Andrew, looking at the Arms of the High Cross. Handing his Cloak to the Soldier he was lifted up on to his tree of Life.*

D3a
A conventionalised rose.

D4a
The arms and badge of King Edward IV. The King came to Wells on the 11th of April 1470, in pursuit of Warwick the Kingmaker. The design, together with the design on D7a, is taken from a carved stone panel above the entrance to the George Inn, Glastonbury, which was built by Abbot Selwood in 1475. The King's badge, a *rose en soleil* can be seen on D1. (The Dean's Embroidery).

D5a
The initials of Bishop Thomas Cornish (a T and C encircling a sheaf of corn), is taken from a shield on his tomb by the entrance to the Chapter House steps. Another shield on his tomb shows his rebus, the heads of three Cornish choughs and three sheaves of corn. The background is patterned with ears and sheaves of corn and the Cornish chough. Thomas Cornish was suffragan bishop from 1493-1513 during the episcopates of Bishops Fox, King and Hadrian. At the same time, he was Chancellor, then Precentor of Wells Cathedral, Prior of St John's Hospital, Wells, Vicar of St Cuthbert's Church, Wells and other parishes and also Provost of Oriel College, Oxford.

D7a
Back The Shield of St George. As with D4a, this design is taken from a carved stone panel at the George Inn at Glastonbury. George was brought up in a Christian family in Cappadocia. At the age of fourteen, when his father died, he presented himself to Emperor Diocletian at Nicomedia and successfully applied for a post as a soldier, soon to be promoted. In 302, Diocletian ordered the arrest of all Christian soldiers and insisted that they should offer a sacrifice to pagan gods. Despite the offer of many bribes George refused, and was tortured and beheaded. He was canonised by Pope Gelasius in 494. When Edward III formed the Order of the Garter in 1350, he made Saint George the Patron Saint of England. The Cross of St George forms the national flag of England.

Seat The Heralds' badge of England and the Rose of St George.

D8a

D9a

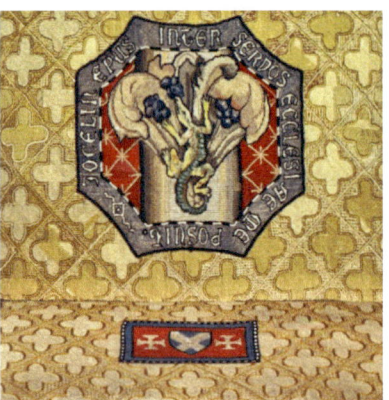
D10a

D11a

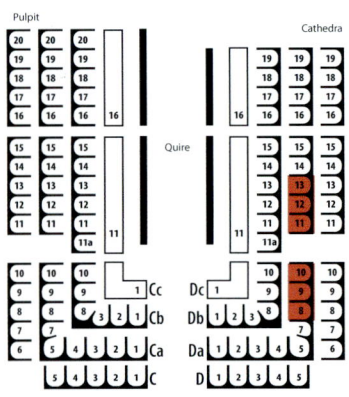

D12a

D13a

D8a

Duck rising from reeds. The motto around the ducks says *I come here from the Bishop's Moat*. Records show that ducks were kept on the moat for many centuries.

D9a

Swans on the palace moat. Swans were highly esteemed in the Middle Ages. In 1349, King Edward III appeared at a tournament accompanied by a swan. With the motto *Hay, Hay, the Whythe Swan*.

D10a

Lizard from the carving on a shaft near the entrance to the Chapter House steps. With the motto - *Bishop Jocelyn placed me among the servants of this Cathedral*. (See C17a – Bishop Jocelyn).

D11a

An angel with a trumpet. The design is adapted from stained glass in the north window of the Lady Chapel.

D12a

The arms of the see surrounded by semée fourteenth century florets.

D13a

Athelm. The first Bishop of Wells 909 -914. In 905 Pope Formosus complained to King Edward the Elder that the West Saxons had been without a bishop for seven years and that if this was not rectified he would lay a curse on the English, instead of the blessing which Pope Gregory had sent them. After consultation with the Archbishop of Canterbury, and with the Pope's agreement, the sees of Winchester and Sherborne were subdivided to make five sees out of two. The new sees were Ramsbury, Crediton and Wells. Athelm was a Somerset man who had been a monk at Glastonbury and was a relative of St Dunstan. He was translated to Canterbury in 914. In his embroidery he is seen wearing a pallium (see the side panels of the throne). He died in 923 and is buried at Canterbury.

D14a

D15a

D16a

D17a

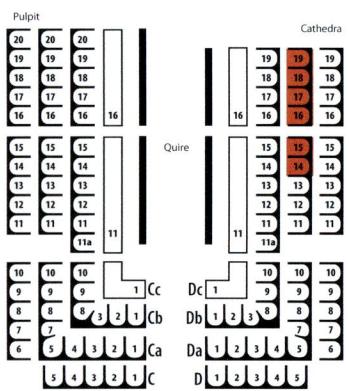

D18a

D19a

D14a

Arms of the see, as D12a.

D16a

Saint Dunstan was a relative of Athelm. He received his early education at Glastonbury. When Athelm became Archbishop in 916, Dunstan followed him to Canterbury and joined the household of King Athelstan. Dunstan was ordained, but was very unpopular at court, being seen as too pious. After Athelstan died in 939, there was a succession of kings and Dunstan spent two years in a monastery at Ghent. By 957 the political climate had changed. Edgar became King and Dunstan returned to England to become Bishop of Worcester, then Bishop of London. He resigned both these sees when he became Archbishop of Canterbury in 959, but he managed to remain Abbot of Glastonbury for some years. Dunstan was a talented craftsman whose skills included ironwork, painting, lyre playing, writing, poetry and embroidery (including altar cloths, and vestments). The centre of the seat back shows him giving a piece of embroidery to a lady for her to stitch. The medallions on each side depict a legend about Dunstan resisting the Devil. On the left is the Devil and on the right, Dunstan with tongs heated in a furnace, with which he will tweak the Devil's nose. The design is taken from the fourteenth century Luttrell Psalter.

D18a

King Ina was King of Wessex, 688-726. Ina was a Christian king who ruled as a patron and protector of the church. In 705 he gave the land for a great Minster church to be built by the wells and is remembered in Wells Cathedral by a stone in the floor in the east end of the nave which was placed there at the instigation of Dean Armitage Robinson. The stone reads *Ina Rex* and *Vetusta ecclesia* or old -ancient church. He built a castle at Taunton. Towards the end of his life the people were rebellious and he abdicated. He and his wife left England and travelled as pilgrims to Rome, where they lived in humility. He died there in 726. His name is written in Celtic script on his embroidery.

D15a

An angel with a trumpet, as D11a.

D17a

Saint Aldhelm's Cross. Aldhelm was born around 640 and was a relative of King Ina. He is said to have encouraged the King to build a church at Glastonbury. He was educated at Canterbury, and became a Benedictine monk. By the 670s he became Abbot of Malmesbury. He was a learned man in both Greek and Latin, and scholars from as far away as Scotland and France sought his advice. Aldhelm loved music, and when he became Bishop of Sherborne in 705, he found people unwilling to listen to preaching, so he stood on a busy bridge, played his harp and sang sacred songs to the crowd (see C8a and the right hand side panel of the throne). As bishop he was diligent in his responsibilities and travelled round the diocese visiting parishes. He died suddenly in the church at Doulting in 709. Seven commemorative stone crosses were erected to mark the resting places on the long journey to Malmesbury, where he is buried. The design on the embroidery is based on a piece of one of the crosses which is kept at the Royal Literary and Scientific Institute in Bath.

D19a

Saint Aldhelm's Cross (asD17a).

C20a

C19a

C18a

C17a

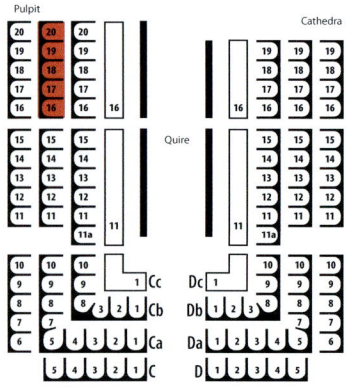
C16a

C20a and C16a

Cross Fitchée. These crosses had pointed ends enabling the pilgrims to fix them in the ground whilst they performed their devotions. It is also thought that they may have been processional crosses which could be placed in sockets on the Altar.

C18a

Polydore Vergil, Archdeacon of Wells, 1508-54. Polydore, an Italian academic and writer, came to England in 1502 as Collector of Peter's Pence. His compatriot, Cardinal Hadrian de Castello (see D10a), became Bishop of Bath and Wells in 1504, and as he did not come to Wells, Polydore acted as his proxy at the enthronement. Polydore was made Archdeacon of Wells in 1508 and he undertook duties delegated to him by Hadrian. In 1505, Henry VII commissioned Polydore to write a history of England, which was published in 1534. His treatment of legendary histories, especially that of Joseph of Arimathea, caused some indignation. Falling out of favour with Wolsey, who had intercepted his letters to Hadrian containing derogatory remarks about him, Polydore was imprisoned in the Tower. He had presented magnificent stall hangings for the quire of the Cathedral. The embroidery shows the arms of the see in the centre of a laurel tree, and above, the words, *These are the gifts of Polydore Vergil, I am the Laurel, the honour of Excellence, a delight in time of triumph…*

C19a

Reginald, Bishop of Bath, 1174-91. In 1162 Henry II appointed Thomas Becket Archbishop of Canterbury and Reginald joined his staff. As the King's relations with Becket deteriorated, Reginald supported him and Becket angrily excommunicated Reginald. To expiate Becket's murder in 1170, the King sent Reginald to Chartreuse to persuade Hugh of Avalon to take charge of Witham, a Carthusian establishment which he had founded. This event is illustrated in the left-hand oval of the embroidery. The motto around it reads, *The Isles have need of thee*. To reward his success Reginald was made Bishop of Bath. The centre oval shows Reginald's seal. The right hand oval shows Reginald at the coronation of Richard I. Ever since that time the Bishop of Bath and Wells has traditionally supported the monarch on the left side at his/her coronation. Reginald started building the present Cathedral in 1175.

C17a

Jocelyn, Bishop of Bath and Glastonbury, 1206-1219 and of Bath, 1219-42, was born and brought up in Somerset and is described as *totus Wellensis*. He and his brother Hugh (later Bishop of Lincoln) were friends and advisors to King John, who often disregarded their advice. The King objected to the Pope's choice of Stephen Langton as Archbishop of Canterbury, and in 1208 the Pope retaliated by putting England under Interdict, closing all churches and suspending services. The next year the Pope excommunicated King John, and Jocelyn, Hugh and four other bishops went into voluntary exile in France. Jocelyn probably acquired his Limoges crozier during this time. It is in the Cathedral library and is also depicted on the right side of the throne embroidery. The King gave in, the bishops returned and the Interdict ended in 1213. Jocelin was a builder, and in 1220, after a long delay he restarted work on the nave and west front of the Cathedral. The embroidery shows, in the centre, Jocelyn's private seal; on the right, he is praying with SS Andrew and John, with the Blessed Virgin and Child above. On the left, the west front, dedicated in 1239.

C15a

C14a

C13a

C12a

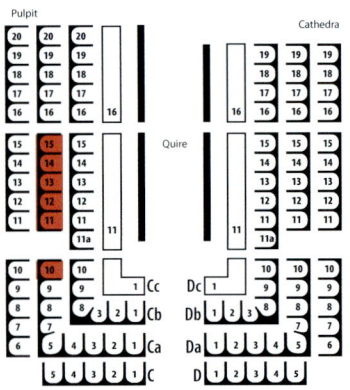

C11a

C10a

C15a

Saint Joseph of Arimathea arriving at Glastonbury. This embroidery shows Saint Joseph with the Tor in the background. The figure of the saint is taken from fifteenth century stained glass at Langport Church. According to legend, St Philip sent a team of twelve disciples, led by St Joseph, to England to teach Christianity. After a difficult journey, King Arviragus rejected their message, but gave them the island of Yniswitrin (the Glassy Isle), where they built a wattle church dedicated to Mary. Bordering the embroidery, is the Glastonbury thorn, said to have grown from St Joseph's staff, which he thrust into the ground at Wirrall Hill. The thorn blooms around Christmas time, and it is recorded that Bishop Montague (D17) gave a bunch in flower to Queen Anne, consort of James I, on Christmas Day.

C13a

The Arms of Saint Joseph of Arimathea (traditional). Legend tells that Joseph brought with him to Glastonbury, "two cruets", containing the blood and sweat of Jesus. In the background is the holy thorn.

C14a and C12a

The leaden cross from King Arthur's tomb at Glastonbury. In 1191, the Abbey monks announced the discovery of the tomb of Arthur and Guinevere. Edward I and Queen Eleanor saw the tomb on a state visit in 1278. Leland says he handled and measured the cross and it was illustrated by Camden in "Britannia" in 1607. The inscription on the cross reads, *Here lies interred in the Isle of Avalon the renowned King Arthur*.

C11a

The arms of Glastonbury Abbey. John of Glastonbury's *Historie* relates that as King Arthur was worshipping at the Shrine of St Mary Magdalene at Beckery near Glastonbury, he had a vision of Our Lady with Jesus in her arms. As a memento, she gave him a crystal cross and *passed out of sight*. To honour this, Arthur changed his arms, which had previously been silver with three red lions, to green with a silver cross and an image of Our Lady and Jesus over the right arm of the Cross. The Holy Thorn is in the background.

C10a

Angels with instruments of music and chants. The design was adapted from Queen Mary's Psalter, a beautiful illuminated fourteenth century manuscript, thought to be the work of Saint Augustine's Abbey at Canterbury. It once belonged to Mary Tudor, to whom it was given by a customs officer who saved it from being taken abroad. The psalter is kept at the British Museum.

C9a

C8a

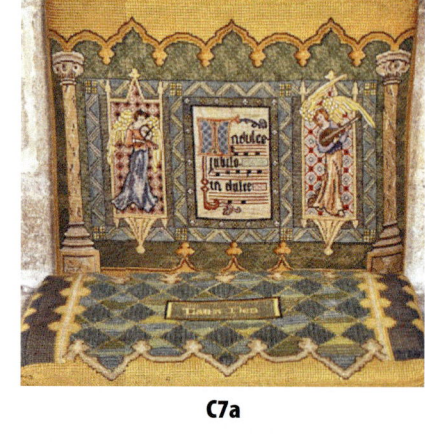

C7a

C5a

C4a

C9a

Saint Indract (and chant). Saint Indract came over from Ireland at the time of King Ina, and established a cell at Glastonbury. John of Glastonbury tells in his Chronicle that Indract found wild celery (*apium graveolens*) growing at the foot of the Polden Hills. Wanting to introduce wild celery to Ireland, he provided the brothers with white linen bags and they set off to collect seed. On the way back to Glastonbury it was late and they decided to spend the night at Shapwick.

Some of King Ina's soldiers saw them, and, thinking that their bags were full of gold, killed them. On the embroidery in the medallion, Saint Indract, with his bag on his waist, is gathering celery seeds. In the border around the chant one can see soldiers with bows and arrows. The chant reads, *All ye green things upon the earth - bless ye the Lord*. Saint Indract was buried at Glastonbury.

C8a

Saint Aldhelm with his harp (and chant). See also throne right side and D17a. St Aldhelm loved music, and when he became Bishop of Sherborne in 705, he found that people were unwilling to listen to preaching, so he stood on a busy bridge where he played his harp and sang sacred songs to the crowd, enticing them to follow him into the church. The words of the chant are *O praise God in his holiness, praise him upon the lute and harp*.

C7a

Angels with instruments of music and chant. See C10a. The design of this embroidery is also taken from Queen Mary's Psalter.

C5a

Pomegranates. The badge of Queen Mary Tudor was derived from that of her mother, Queen Katherine of Aragon. The design depicts pomegranates.

C4a

Lilies. These lilies of conventionalised seventeenth century design, were taken from Louisa Pesel's notebook. The introduction of canvas work embroideries in churches and cathedrals was started by Miss Pesel in Winchester in the early 1930s. When Bishop Woods, an old friend, became Bishop of Winchester, she embroidered cushions and kneelers for his bare-looking private chapel. These were seen by the Dean of Winchester who wanted similar embroideries in Winchester Cathedral. They were also seen by Dean Malden of Wells, who wished to reintroduce medieval colour to Wells Cathedral. Gloucester, Salisbury and Worcester Cathedrals followed suit.

C3a

C2a

C1a

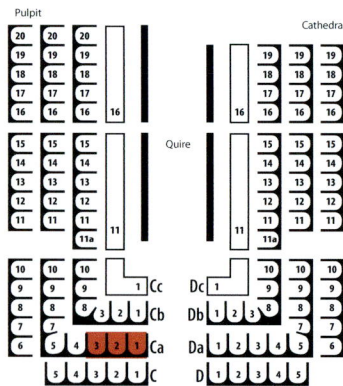

42

C3a

The vision of Saint Stephen. The centre panel of the embroidery shows Saint Stephen being stoned to death. Saint Stephen is the patron saint of stonemasons and the background is covered with masons' marks which can be seen around Wells Cathedral. The hymn around the panel is by Adam de Saint Victor and it reads, *Plenus Sancto Spiritu Penetrat intuit Stephanus coelestia Videns Dei gloriam*.

C2a

The Blessed Virgin adoring the Holy Child. An adapted copy of this embroidery hangs in the Chapel of the Bishop's Palace, on the back of which there is an explanation. The building in the background is the Bishop's Palace, the tree is the Glastonbury thorn, the rustic footbridge is built over the moat (the water which comes from the springs which give Wells its name). The emblems in the background differ as does the word beneath the centre medallion. The cathedral reads *Magnificat* and the Bishop's Chapel version reads *Emmanuel*.

C1a

Lilies from Louisa Pesel's notebook. As C4a.

D1b

D2b

D3b

D8b

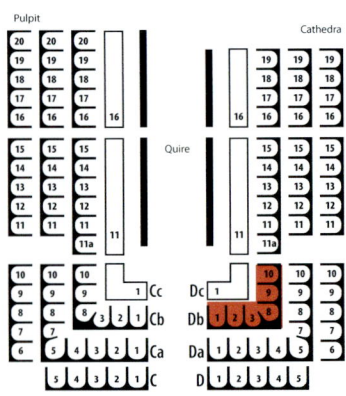

D9b

D10b

D1b
A design adapted from a seventeenth century sampler.

D2b
The Cross of Saint Andrew the Martyr. The Cathedral is dedicated to Saint Andrew, and his saltire cross forms the arms of the see of Bath and Wells. Saint Andrew refused to be crucified on a cross similar to that of Jesus, saying that he was unworthy to be so greatly honoured. The Cross is supported by an angel and the motto, *Haec Sancti Andreae Martiris Crux*, which translated from Latin reads, 'This is the cross of Saint Andrew the Martyr'.

D3b
As D1b - A design adapted from a seventeenth century sampler.

D8b
Columbines. A design adapted from a fourteenth century psalter.

D9b
Roses entwined with the words *Laus Deo*.

D10b
As D8b Columbines. A design adapted from a fourteenth century psalter.

Db11a

D11b

D12b

D13b

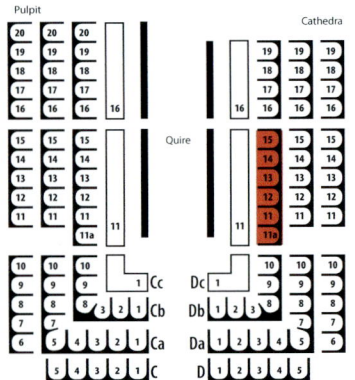

D14b

D15b

Db11a

Back. With the introduction of polyphony, it became a "Rector's" job to direct a choir using a choir book on a lectern. Psalm 97 letter "C" is depicted from a French painting *c*. 1320/25.

Seat. This 13th century antiphonal by the Master of Gerona for the feast of St Nicholas on 6th December. The Saint is bringing gold dowries for two daughters of an unhappy father!

D12b

Back Figures of three Vicars Choral in niches similar to those on the west front.

Seat The opening bars of "Starre Anthem" *Almighty God who by the leading of a star*, by Dr. John Bull of Wellow near Bath. He was organist to the Chapel Royal in 1591 and became organist in Antwerp Cathedral in 1613. He claimed to have written *God save the King* but two manuscripts, one containing this composition, disappeared. Described as 'the Liszt of his age', he died in 1628 and is buried in Antwerp.

D14b

Back Three figures of Vicars Choral shown in niches like those on the west front (as D11b back).

Seat The opening bars of the anthem *Glory be to the Father* by C.W. Lavington, Cathedral organist, 1850-92.

D11b

Back Illuminated text, with the words *God be the Guide and the work will here abide*. There is a border of flowers around the text, which has been adapted from an illuminated manuscript psalter by Petrus Monoculus, and which is in the Cathedral Library.

Seat This is a mosaic in the floor of an early basilica at Bethlehem. It was found, covered in ashes, after a fire, around 525 and is thought to be older than that.

All four designs chosen by Neil Bonham from the Ludwig Collection now in the J Paul Getty Museum

D13b

Back Angels praising the Lord. This design is taken from stained glass which can be seen in the tracery in the Beauchamp Chapel at Saint Mary's Church at Warwick.

Seat The opening bars of the anthem *O for a faith that will not shrink* by D.D.R. Pouncey, who was Cathedral organist, 1936-70.

D15b

Back Illuminated text *Gloria in excelsis Deo - Gloria* (as D11b back).

Seat Cross of Saint Andrew from stained glass formerly in a room over the west cloister.

D16b

D17b

D18b

D19b

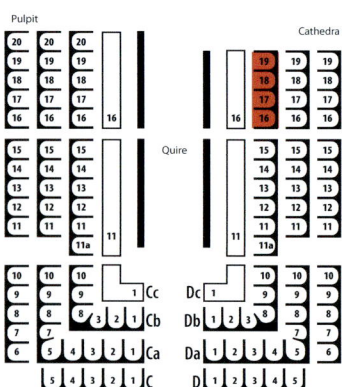

D16b

The tree of life. The design is adapted from a fragment of Anglo-Saxon stone carving, perhaps part of a foliated cross, found near Kelston Church, and now built into the chancel wall.

D17b

King Alfred's Harp. King Alfred had been defeated by the Danes on several occasions. He was a talented harpist, and the story goes that when he entered the enemy camp disguised as a minstrel to entertain them, he overheard their battle plans. As a result of this, Alfred's army were well prepared for the next battle at Edington in 878, and finally beat the Danes.

D18b

King Alfred at Wedmore in 878. Having been defeated by Alfred's army, the Danes were besieged, desperate, hungry and frightened. They promised to leave Wessex and their king, Guthrum, and thirty of his senior men requested baptism. Three weeks later they were baptised at Aller. The following week, they went to Wedmore for "chrism loosing", or removal of the baptismal gown, and the Peace of Wedmore was signed. Two months later the Danes withdrew to Cirencester.

D19b

The tree of life (as D16b).

C20b
The figure of a canon taken from an alabaster panel on the tomb in Saint Calixtus Chapel.

C19b
Cross bottonée with semée of Ranworth sprays.

C18b
The Annunciation, also taken from the alabaster panel on the tomb in Saint Calixtus Chapel.

C17b
Cross bottoneé (as C19b).

C16b
The figure of a canon (as C20b).

C15b
Back The Arms of the see of Bath and Wells, with the words *Let thy blessing O God be upon the Cathedral Church in Wells*. (As C11b but with variation in text).

Seat The Cross of Saint Andrew (as D11b).

C14b

C13b

C12b

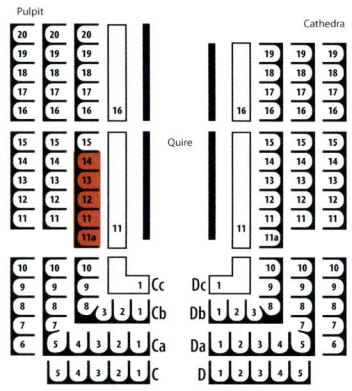

C11b

Cb11a

52

C14b

Back A chant with angels holding musical instruments, taken from the Luttrell Psalter. The chant reads *Credo quad redemptor meus in vivit*. ('I live because my redeemer liveth').

Seat The opening bars of a chant by Percy Buck, organist,1896-99, *The Lord is good to all*. He did much to promote the theological students' knowledge of music. The Chapter thought highly of him and contributed towards the expenses of his D.Mus. degree. He received a knighthood in 1936.

C12b

Back Instruments of music. The embroidery is headed with the words, *Praise the Lord with the harp, sing praises to him with the lute and instrument of ten strings*. (Psalm 33 v.2). Around the sides are the harp, cittern, psaltery and lute. In the centre is the figure of an angel with a cittern.

Seat A setting *We praise Thee O God* by the Reverend T.H. Davis, who became organist at Wells Cathedral in 1899 and graduated D.Mus. the following year. In 1912, he was appointed Prebendary, and in 1920, Precentor and Residentiary Canon. He retired as organist in 1933 but continued as Precentor until his death in 1947. He was the only organist to be promoted in this way.

C11b

Back The arms of the see of Bath and Wells (as C15b but with a differing text). The text reads *Let thy blessing O God be upon all who minister and worship in this Cathedral Church of Saint Andrew of Wells*.

Seat The cross of Saint Andrew (as C15b).

C13b

Back Instruments of music. There are a number of musical instruments in the four corners of the embroidery including, trumpets, waterman's horn, serpent and brass horn, recorder, shawm, flageolet and horn. At the top, the words, *At the altar, one hundred and twenty priests sounding with trumpets*. In the centre is the badge of the Somerset Light Infantry, a crown above bugle.

Seat The opening bars of an anthem *I will arise and go to my father*, by Robert Creyghton, who was Precentor of Wells Cathedral, 1674-1734. He was the son of Robert Creyghton, whom he accompanied abroad when the latter was chaplain to Charles II in exile. At the Reformation Robert Creyghton senior became Dean of Wells, then from 1670-72, Bishop of Bath and Wells. In the introduction to Wells Cathedral Chapter Act Book 1666, p.xvi, the Precentor's music is described as *undistinguished, pedestrian and sadly lacking in melodic invention*. He died in 1734 aged 96.

Cb11a

Back. The image of the letter C at the beginning of Psalm 97 - *Cantate Domino canticum novum*, "Sing unto the Lord a new song", shows King David (who wrote the Psalms) playing a carillon of bells with musicians on the viol and the horn after a c. 1215/20 French Master.

Seat. 13th Century antiphonal floral "C" (from an unknown artist) for the fourth Sunday in Advent, *canite tuba in Sion*, "Blow the trumpet in Sion".

C10b

C9b

C8b

C3b

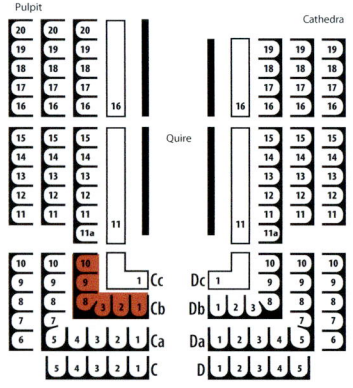

C2b

C1b

C10b

Conventionalised honeysuckle. The design is taken from a seventeenth century sampler.

C9b

Conventionalised pinks. This embroidery design has been adapted from Susan Ingram's sampler of 1700.

C8b

Conventionalised honeysuckle. As C10b.

C3b

Arms of the see of Bath and Wells.

C2b

Back Wells Cathedral Clock, with the inscription *Sphericus archetypum globus hic monstrat microcosm*, which means, This round ball denotes the archetypal microcosm, i.e. man.

Seat This design is adapted from the pavement laid down in front of the High Altar of Westminster Abbey by Abbot Ware in 1263. The centre ball symbolises the universe and its duration is foretold. The inscription reads *Sphericus archetypum globus hic monstrat macrocosm*. The Westminster version means, more correctly, 'This round ball denotes the universe, its archetype'. The moon is waxing and waning in the centre, and the four winds in the corners all seem to point to the macro cosmic system being referred to. (R.P. Howgrave-Graham).

C1b

The arms of the see (as C3b).

D1c Back

D3c Back

D1c–D10c

C1c Back

C10c–C1c

D11c-D15c

D16c-D19c

C20c-C16c

C15c-C11c

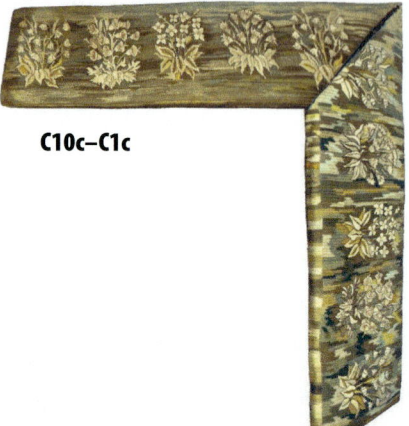

Runners

D1c Back
Head Virger's seat, embroidered c.1999 with conventionalised plants.

D3c Back
Virger's seat, embroidered c.2010 with conventionalised plants.

D1c-D10c
Cushions on corner seat Conventionalised plants in a fifteenth century design.

D11c–D15c
Continuous runner for choristers. Vine scroll on yellow background.

D16c-D19c
Continuous runner . Semeé of sprigs of flowers, adapted from fourteenth century painted Rood screen in Saint Helen's Church, Ranworth, Norfolk.

C20c–C16c
Continuous runner. Semeé of sprigs of flowers (as D16c – D19c).

C15c-C11c
Continuous runner for choristers. Vine scroll on yellow background.

C1c Back
Virger's seat (embroidered c.1995).

C10c–C1c
Cushions on corner seat. Conventionalised plants, fifteenth century design.

Row 1

Row 2

Row 3

Row 4

Row 5

Row 6

Row 7

Row 8

Row 9

Row 10

High Altar Communion Rail Kneeler

Sedilia Seat

Presbytery Runners

South side from entrance to south quire aisle

Row 1. Vine with bird (short seat).

Row 2. Vine with two birds. Made in 1990s to replace a runner which was stolen (short seat).

Row 3. Vine with grapes and birds. (Seat is a little longer than 1 and 2).

Row 4. Roses in geometrical design (long seat).

Row 5. Acorn design with Saint Andrew's Cross in the centre (long seat).

Row 6. Vine with bird (short seat).

Row 7. Arms of monastic houses of Somerset with a pomegranate design in the background (long seat). (left to right) Templecombe, Stavordale, Bruton, Barlinch, Athelney, Taunton, Cleeve, Glastonbury, Dunster.

Row 8. Arms of knights of the shire (long seat).(left to right) Sir John St Loe (1297), Sir Peter d'Every (1307), Sir Hugh Luttrell (1404), Sir Giles Daubeney (1478), Sir Amyas Paulet (1495), Sir Nicholas Wadham (1524), Sir Edward Waldegrave (1559), Sir Thomas Horner (1584), Sir Hugh Portman (1597), Admiral Blake (1656) Sir William Wyndham (1708).

Row 9. Roses in geometrical design (long seat).

Row 10. Arms of monastic houses of Somerset with a vine pattern in the background (long seat). (left to right) Buckland, Glastonbury, Mulcheney, Courtnay Worspring (Woodspring), Bath, Cannington Couci, Witham, Hinton Charterhouse and Keynsham.

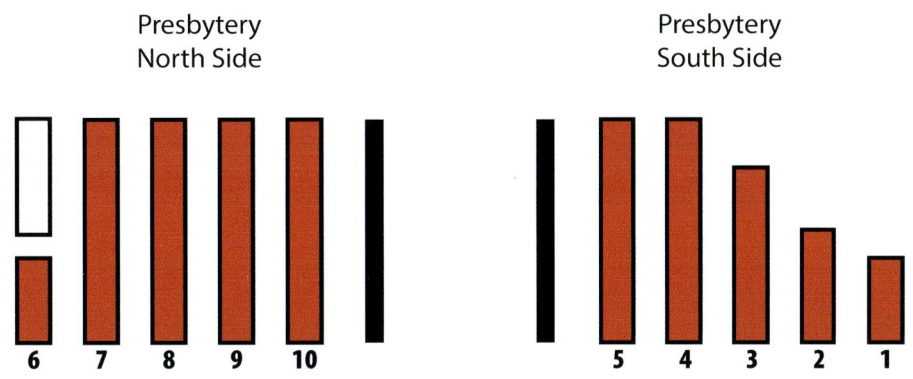

Needleworkers who stitched the Embroideries

The Throne

The throne centre panel: Mrs. Leonora Jenner.   Side panels: Miss Mildred Alice Carr.   Desk cushion: Miss Elizabeth Underhill.

The Hangings

D1	The Dean: Miss Wigram.		C20	The Archdeacon of Bath: Mrs. Leonora Jenner.
D2	The Archdeacon of Taunton: Mrs. Gill.		C19	The Treasurer: Mrs. Leonora Jenner.
D3	Bishop Drokensford: Miss Cheetham.		C18	Bishop Laud: Miss Child.
D4	Bishop Harewell: Mrs. Pelly.		C17	Bishop Lake: Miss Mildred Alice Carr.
D5	Bishop Bubwith: Mrs. Thompson.		C16	Bishop Curle: Mrs. Kewley.
D6	Bishop Bekynton: The Reverend J.J. Antrobus.		C15	Bishop Creyghton: Mrs. Scott.
D7	Bishop Stillington: Mrs. Shaw Mellor.		C14	Bishop Mews: Rev. and Mrs. E.P. Luxford.
D8	Bishop Fox: Girls of Bishop Fox's School.		C13	Bishop Ken: Miss Isabel Jones.
D9	Bishop King: Mrs. Shaw Mellor.		C12	Bishop Kidder: Mrs. Leonora Jenner.
D10	Cardinal Hadrian de Castello: Kenneth Stubbs.		C11	Bishop Hooper : Miss Bockholt.
D11	Cardinal Wolsey: Kenneth Stubbs.		C10	Bishop Willes: F.J. Child, M.D.
D12	Bishop Knight: Mrs. Jackson.		C9	Bishop Wynne: Mrs. Scott.
D13	Bishop Barlow: Mrs. Drago Montagu.		C8	Bishop Beadon: Rev. J.J. Antrobus.
D14	Bishop Bourne: Mrs. Leybourne Popham.		C7	Bishop Law: Miss Mildred Alice Carr.
D15	Bishop Berkeley: The Reverend J.J. Antrobus.		C6	Bishop Bagot : Lady Wickham.
D16	Bishop Still: Mrs. Aldworth.		C5	Bishop Eden: Mrs. Hugh Foster.
D17	Bishop Montagu: Mrs. Leybourne Popham.		C4	Bishop Hervey: Miss Symonds.
D18	The Chancellor: The Reverend J.J. Antrobus.		C3	Bishop Kennion: Rev. E.P. Luxford.
D19	The Archdeacon of Wells: Miss G.I. Sherston.		C2	Bishop Wynne Willson: Mrs. Bates Harbin.
			C1	The Precentor: Mrs. Jackson.

The Decani Seats and Backs. Row a.

- **D1a** Conventionalised rose, *Back* Miss Avice Guiness. *Seat* Miss E. Rocke.
- **D2a** Vision of Saint Andrew. *Back* Lady Hylton and Mrs. Jackson. *Seat* Mrs. C.N. Brown.
- **D3a** Conventionalised rose. *Back* Miss Avice Guiness. *Seat* Mrs. Keen.
- **D4a** Arms and badge of King Edward IV. *Back* Mrs. Douglas MacLean. *Seat* Mrs. Drago Montagu.
- **D5a** Rebus of Bishop Cornish. *Back* Mrs. Chase and Miss Dorothea Nicholson. *Seat* Mrs. Godden.
- **D7a** Shield of Saint George. *Back* Begun by Miss E. Rocke and finished by Mrs. W.H. Bond. *Seat* Mrs. Claude Neville.
- **D8a** Duck rising from reeds. *Back* Mrs. Drago Montagu. *Seat* Miss J. Butler.
- **D9a** Swans on the Palace Moat. *Back* Miss Mildred A. Carr. *Seat* Miss Mildred A. Carr.
- **D10a** Lizard from carving. *Back* Mrs. Drago Montagu. *Seat* Mrs. Drago Montagu.
- **D11a** Angel with trumpet. *Back* Miss Isabel Jones. *Seat* Mrs. J. Antrobus.
- **D12a** Arms of the See. *Back* Mrs. Roger Evans. *Seat* Mrs. Wadham.
- **D13a** Bishop Athelm. *Back* Mr. Christopher Wade. *Seat* Mrs. Francis Parish.
- **D14a** Arms of the See. *Back* Miss Eve Ferguson and finished by Mrs. Horsburgh. *Seat* Mrs. Keen.
- **D15b** Angel with trumpet. *Back* Miss G.I. Sherston. *Seat* Mrs. A. Foster.
- **D16a** Saint Dunstan. *Back* Mrs. Roger Evans. *Seat* Miss Handsley.
- **D17a** Saint Aldhelm's Cross. *Back* Mrs. Edmund Jackson. *Seat* Miss C. Street.
- **D18a** King Ina. *Back* Mrs. Whale. *Seat* Miss Mildred A. Carr.
- **D19a** Saint Aldhelm's Cross. *Back* Mrs. Hugh Foster. *Seat* Mrs. Cyprian Webb.

The Cantoris Seats and Backs. Row a.

- **C20a** Cross Fitchée. *Back* Miss E. Woodhouse. *Seat* Mrs. Wadham.
- **C19a** Bishop Reginald. *Back* Miss Meline Ferguson. *Seat* Mrs. Keen.
- **C18a** Polydore Vergil. *Back* Mrs. Bates Harbin. *Seat* Miss Abbott.
- **C17a** Bishop Jocelyn. *Back* Mrs. Malcolm Venables. *Seat* Mrs. Keen.
- **C16a** Cross Fitchée. *Back* Mrs. Gould and Mrs. Thornton. *Seat* Miss Lilian Whitby.
- **C15a** St Joseph of Arimathea arriving at Glastonbury. *Back* Medallion: Lady Hylton and Miss Vernon, background Mrs. Codrington. *Seat* Mrs. Codrington.
- **C14a** Leaden cross from King Arthur's tomb at Glastonbury. *Back* Mrs. Laws. *Seat* Miss F. Rees-Mogg.
- **C13a** Arms of Joseph of Arimathea. *Back* Mrs. Edmund Jackson. *Seat* Mrs. Drago Montagu.
- **C12a** Leaden cross from King Arthur's tomb at Glastonbury. *Back* Mrs. A. Foster. *Seat* Mrs. A. Foster.
- **C11a** Arms of Glastonbury Abbey. *Back* Dowager Lady Sysonby. *Seat* Miss Frances Berryman.
- **C10a** Angels with instruments. *Back* Mrs. Jackson of Holton. *Seat* Mrs. Keen.
- **C9a** Saint Indract. *Back* Mrs. Edmund Jackson. *Seat* Mrs. Wythes and Miss J Gayford.
- **C8a** Saint Ealdhelm with harp. *Back* Chant: Lady Phipps, Medallion: Lady Hylton, Border: Mr K. Stubbs. *Seat* Mrs. Keen.
- **C7a** Angels with instruments. *Back* Mrs. Edmund Jackson. *Seat* Miss Letticia Bond.
- **C5a** Pomegranate design. *Back*: facing east: Miss Willcox: facing south: Miss K. Hope. *Seat* Mrs. Keen, Lady Hylton.
- **C4a** Lilies. *Back* Miss Lilian Whitby. *Seat* Miss H. Greene.
- **C3a** Vision of St Stephen. *Back* Medallion: Lady Hylton *Background*: Miss Underhill. *Seat* The Rev. G.A.A. Wright.
- **C2a** Adoration. *Back* Miss E. Cheetham. *Seat* Mrs. Aldridge.
- **C1a** Lilies. *Back* Miss E. Cheetham. *Seat* Miss H. Greene.

The Decani Seats and Backs. Row b.

D1b Design from 17th century sampler. *Back* Miss Abbott. *Seat* Miss D. Nicholson.

D2b Cross of St Andrew: Martyr. *Back* Lady Hylton *Background*: Mrs. Fowles. *Seat* Lady Kennard.

D3b Design from 17th century sampler. *Back* Miss C. Jervis. *Seat* Mrs. H.S. Urch.

D8b Columbines. *Back* Dowager Lady Ampthill. *Seat* Mrs. Claude Neville.

D9b Roses entwined. *Back* Miss Mildred Carr. *Seat* Mrs. Wadham.

D10b Columbines. *Back* Miss C. Stanhope. *Seat* Miss Bittlestone.

Db11a *Back* Conductor and figures. Carolyn Partleton and Marion Robinson. *Seat* Sara Davis and Pauline Herbert.

D11b Illuminated text. *Back* needleworker not known. *Seat* Mosaic Miss Agnes Fry.

D12b Figures of Vicars Choral. *Back* needleworker not known. *Seat* Anthem by Dr John Bull Mrs. C.A. Brocklebank.

D13b Angels. *Back* needleworker not known. *Seat* Anthem by D.D.R. Pouncey Mrs. W.F. Scott.

D14b Figures of Vicars Choral. *Back* needleworker not known. *Seat* Anthem by C.W. Lavington Miss Letitia Bond.

D15b Illuminated text. *Back* needleworker not known. *Seat* Cross of StAndrew Mrs. W.F.Scott.

D16b Tree of Life. *Back* and *Seat* Mrs. A. Foster.

D17b KingAlfred's Harp. *Back* Mrs. Edmund Jackson. *Seat* Mrs. Charles Dodd.

D18b Peace of Wedmore. *Back* Medallion: Miss Stanhope. *Background*: Mrs. A. Foster. *Seat* Mrs. C. Dodd.

D19b Tree of Life. *Back* Mrs. Bernard Bryant. *Seat* Mrs. Lee: Mrs. A. Leche.

The Cantoris Seats and Backs. Row b.

C20b Canon from Boleyn Tomb. *Back* Mrs. Drago Montagu. *Seat* Mrs. Nation.

C19b Cross Bottonée. *Back* Miss Frances Berryman. *Seat* Miss L. Whitby.

C18b Annunciation. *Back* Mrs. Leonora Jenner. *Seat* Miss Mildred Carr.

C17b Cross Bottonée. *Back* Miss Plews. *Seat* Mrs. Needham,

C16b Canon from Boleyn tomb. *Back* Miss Katherine Jones. *Seat* Mrs. Laws.

C15b Arms of the See. *Back* needleworker not known. *Seat* Cross of St Andrew - Girls of Wells High School.

C13b Instruments of music. *Back* needleworker not known. *Seat* Anthem by R. Creyghton, Miss C.A. Brocklebank.

C12b Instruments of music. *Back* needleworker not known. *Seat* Setting by Canon Davis Miss Brownlow.

C11b Arms of the See. *Back* needleworker not known. *Seat* Cross of St Andrew Girls of Wells High School.

Cb11a *Back* King David playing carillon. Dawn Bonham, Alison Baillie and Christopher Jenkins. *Seat* Nancy Long and Christine Webb.

C10b Honeysuckle. *Back* Mrs. Collier. *Seat* Miss E.Rocke.

C9b Conventionalised pinks. *Back* Mrs. Claude Neville. *Seat* Mrs. Claude Neville.

C8b Honeysuckle. *Back* Mrs. Collier. *Seat* Mrs. Keen.

C3b Arms of the See. *Back* Dowager Lady Sysonby. *Seat* Miss R. Brownlow.

C2b Cathedral clock. *Back* Mrs. Charles Dodd and Mrs. Caldwell.

Seat Westminster Abbey pavement Mrs. Burnford

C1b   Arms of the see. *Back* Mrs. Keen. *Seat* Mrs. Drago Montagu and Mrs. Messenger.

The Decani Runners and Backs. Row c.

D1c   *Corner Seat runner. Backs* conventionalised plants. *Head virger's seat* Mrs. M.Jeans (1999). *Virger's seat* Mrs. A Maw (2010). *Seats* Miss Mildred Carr, Mrs. Wadham, Miss Foster and Miss E. Woodhouse.

D11c   *Runner*. Vine scroll on yellow background. *Choristers Seat* Mrs. Campbell Duckworth and Mrs. Hugh Foster.

D16c   *Runner. Ranworth sprays* Miss Barber, Miss Clarke, and Mrs. C. Dodd.

The Cantoris Runners and Backs. Row c.

C16c   *Runner. Ranworth Sprays* Miss Handsley, Mrs. Lovelock, Mrs. A.E.Weatherhead.

C11c   *Runner*. Vine scroll on yellow background. *Choristers seat* Rev. and Mrs. J. Antrobus, Baroness Dimsdale.

C1c   *Corner Seat runner*. Conventionalised plants Mrs. Rawlins. *Virger seat back* Mrs. M. Jeans (1995).

The Presbytery runners-South side (from entrance to south quire aisle)

Row 1   Vine with bird (small seat), Lady Sysonby.

Row 2   Vine with two birds (small seat), Mrs. Mary Ellingworth (1990s).

Row 3   Vine with birds (longer than 1 and 2 but not full length), Miss Whittaker, Mrs. Keen, Mrs. Elderton.

Row 4   Roses in geometrical design (long bench), Mrs. Bates Harbin.

Row 5   Acorn design with St Andrew's Cross (longbench), Miss Avice Guiness, Miss Dorothea Skrine, Mrs. Malet.

The presbytery North side (from entrance to north quire aisle)

Row 6   Vine with birds (small seat), Mrs. Leybourne Popham.

Row 7   Arms of monastic houses of Somerset with pomegranates (long seat), Miss D. Yorke, Mrs. Pelly, Mrs. Lindsay Smith, Rev and Mrs. E.T.P. Luxford.

Row 8   Arms of Knights of the shire (long seat), Mrs. Roger Evans, Miss E. Ingram, Mrs. Tustain.

Row 9   Roses in geometrical design (long seat), Miss Ramsbury, Dr. Bishop, Mrs. Lee and Mrs. Marriott (border).

Row 10   Arms of monastic houses of Somerset with vine pattern (long seat), Mrs. C.F. Chase, Mrs. Quantock Shuldham, Miss Isabel Jones, Mrs. Arthur Leche and Mrs. Eric Wills.

Kneeler for High Altar Communion Rail 1984

Needleworkers not known.

Sedilia seats and backs, 2002

Mary Blundell, Elizabeth Court, Deidre Craven, Sara Davis, Mary Ellingworth, Richard Lewis (Dean), Nancy Long, Pamela Merchant, Florence Miller, Joan Tidball.

Quinque Cope

Mystery and Meaning:
the Millennium Project to replace Altar Frontals and Vestments

Text by the late Richard Lewis, Dean of Wells 1990-2003

This project was intended to stimulate the religious imagination of all those who saw it, and experienced designers tendered for it. Mrs Jane Lemon MBE and Rev Maurice Strike were chosen and the work was carried out by the Sarum Group of Embroiderers and the Royal School of Needlework. Mrs Lemon was founder of the Sarum group, and a teacher and author, and Rev Strike was renowned as an artist, theatre designer, and designer of church fabrics.

There are 63 elements to the project, all financed by public subscription.

Frontals for all six "seasons" of the Church's year. The Nave Altar frontals were designed by Maurice Strike and embroidered by the Royal School of Needlework. They are abstract and diffuse. The High Altar frontals were designed by Jane Lemon and embroidered by the Sarum Group. They are more "formed, strong and clear". Visitors are attracted from Nave to High Altar as pilgrims from darkness to light.

Vestments in colour and fabrics matching for each season. Visually, vestments and frontals make a coherent whole.

Fabrics all bought at the same time so as to avoid problems with textures and dyes. There are leather, beads, theatrical net, hessian and wire, and fabrics and silks from Thailand.

The colours mark the seasons.
- Purple at Advent;
- Silver and gold at Christmas and Easter;
- Hessian sackcloth at Lent;
- Red and yellow for Feast days of the Holy Spirit, including Pentecost and many Saints' Days, Ordination and Confirmation;
- Green for Trinity;
- On Good Friday all frontals are removed and the Altars are left unadorned.

Advent

Subdued, for the beginning of the Christian year, and preparation for Christmas.

At the Nave Altar, the eye is drawn to the centre with the figure on the Cross. At the High Altar the chaos of creation is transformed from darkness to ever-increasing light.

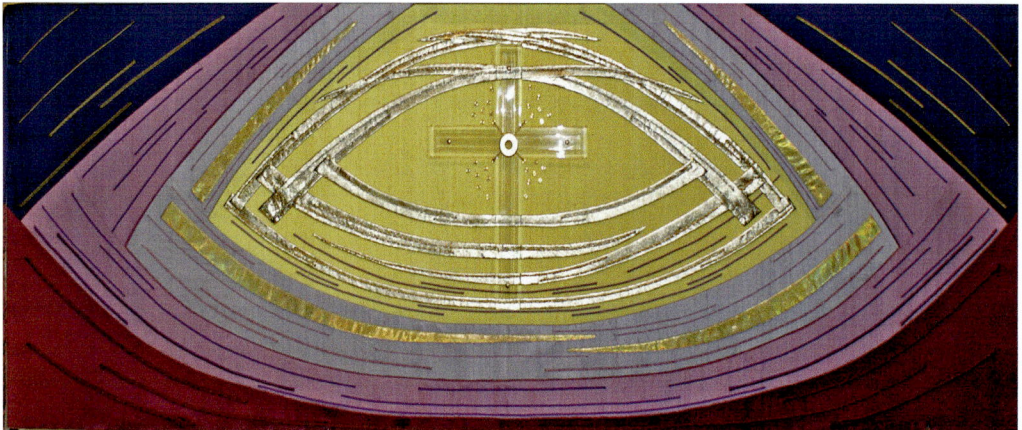

Christmas

At the Nave Altar, "a child is born, a son is given" - the heavens and all creation rejoice. At the High Altar, a star is formed, reflecting the star vault in the Lady Chapel. The star is off-centre - perhaps there is more to come? The robes reflect the abundance of joy of the season.

Lent

Sombre, sackcloth and ashes. A crown of thorns on both frontals; tangled on the Nave Frontal and fully formed on the High Altar. Stark hessian, pulled threadwork, and colour speak of pain and sorrow.

Vestments for Lent also echo the stumbling faith and penitent hearts.

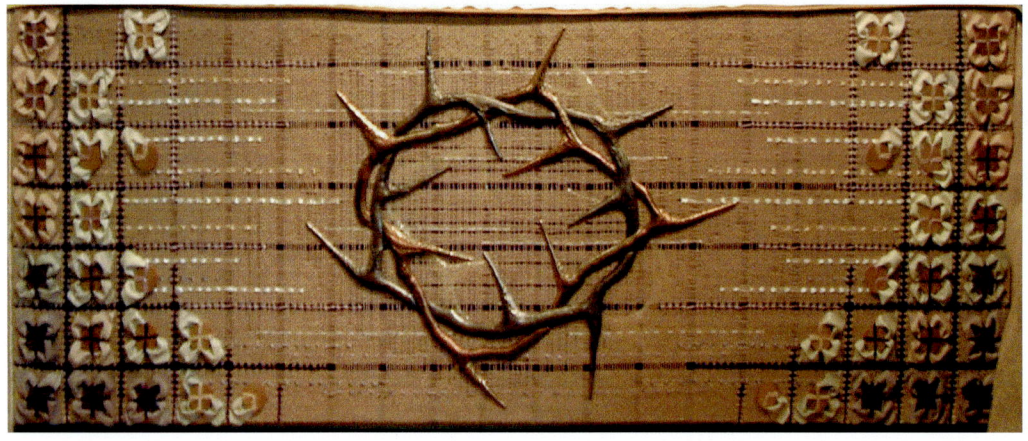

Easter

Reflecting in colour and design the lift of heart and soul - "Christ is Risen" in the Nave and in the Quire, "He is Risen Indeed", echoing the ribs and bosses of the Lady Chapel and Chapter House.

Gold and silver in the vestments signalling the wonder of the day and the appearance of new life. All heaven cries "Glory".

Pentecost

Wind and flames of that day in Jerusalem. Brilliant colours. A hint of the rood on the Scissor Arch above the Nave Frontal. In the Quire, colours the same, the eye is drawn to the glowing centre. The light of life, glowing deep in the hearts of men and women.

Vestments for this day reflect the flames and confusion of the day.

Trinity

This is the "growing season". Filled with light, the Trinity Frontal shows water and fishes, perhaps representing *ichthus*, Latin for fish, early Christians' secret word for Christ.

The plants on the High Altar Frontal continue the theme of calm after the storm.

The celebrant's chasuble reflects the theme described above.

The Chasubles

These are worn by the Chapter of Wells to celebrate the important days and events of the year, each one subtly embodying the colours of one of the seasons.

Advent

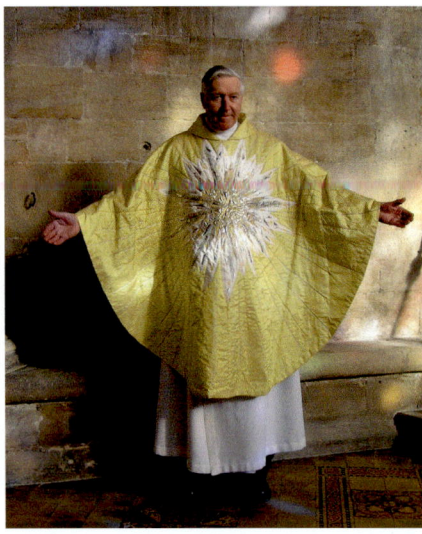

Christmas

Lent

Easter

Pentecost

Pentecost stole

Trinity

Quinque Cope
for the canoons of the cathedral

For further information, see

R. H. Malden, *Hangings in the Quire of Wells Cathedral*. 1948

Alice A. Hylton, *Catalogue of the Canvas Work on the Sub-stalls in the Quire of Wells Cathedral*. 1951 Minutes of the Needleworkers' Meetings.

An article in *Embroidery*, Winter edition 1953/54 by A.H. published by The Embroiderers' Guild

Notes from Lady Hylton's papers prepared by her daughter in law in 1978.

The Quire Embroideries – a guide produced by The Friends of Wells Cathedral (4th revised edition 1985).

Acknowledgements
Michael Blandford and Guides at Wells Cathedral;
Veronica Howe, Cathedral Archivist.

Notes

Notes

Notes